The Magic Bracelet

To order additional copies of this book, contact:
Xlibris
1-888-795-4274
www.Xlibris.com
Orders@Xlibris.com

ISBN: Softcover   978-1-7960-9974-4
        EBook   978-1-7960-9973-7

Print information available on the last page

Rev. date: 04/27/2020

The Magic Bracelet

Ann Allen

Dax was turning and tossing in his sleep; dreaming about his Blue Nose American Bully puppy named Gunnar. Dax was an 11 year old boy with dark blonde hair, big blue eyes and a passion for cars and monster trucks and loved his dog, He sat straight up in bed and looked around his room for Gunnar.

He quickly put on his jeans, hoody and shoes and went into his brother's room.

"Zayne wake up" he said pulling the covers off his brother's bed. "I just know that Gunnar is missing and we have to find him."

Zayne was 2 ½ years younger than Dax and had dark hair, hazel eyes and the most curious mind for a 9 year old. Zayne jumped out of bed and immediately got dressed. They both quietly and silently looked through the house then went outside in the fenced yard.

"Let's don't wake up Mom and Dad. We can go to Gram's house, she'll know what to do." said Dax.

Gram lived 3 houses away on the same street. It was around midnight, no one was around and the street lights shined brightly down on the sidewalk.

"I wished we had gotten a microchip implant for Gunnar from the Vet. The injection only takes minutes then we could have found him through the RFID." said Dax.

"I know Dax. But he does have a collar on with our address and phone number printed on his tag.

What happens if the dogcatcher finds him?" Zayne blurted out.

Dax replied, "Lost and found dogs go to the Animal Shelter or the Humane Society. They will contact us if they find him."

When they got to Gram's front door they both knocked at the same time.

Gram opened the door and said "What a surprise, my grandsons are here!"

Gram had a slender body, long gray hair and always a smile on her face. She was older and wiser and had traveled the world and also lived in many different cities across the USA and in other countries. Dax and Zayne both started talking at the same time.

"Come on in boys. You said Gunnar is missing?" Gram had a puzzled look on her face.

Zayne said, "We looked in the house and in the yard and can't find him."

The boys both plopped down on the leather couch with very disappointing faces and arms folded.

"Ok boys" she said pointing at them. "I have something special to show you, follow me."

The boys followed her into her bedroom. She opened the door to her armoire and took out a small jeweled covered wooden box. When she opened the box a bright green light shot out and glowed on part of the ceiling.

"Wow Gram," said Dax with his mouth opened wide. "What is that?"

"This is a Magic Bracelet," she took it out of the wooden box and put it on her left wrist. "A juju woman in India gave this to me and told me of its secrets. Give me the location of the dog named Gunnar."

The green light got brighter and illuminated a complete address on the bedroom ceiling.

Zayne just stood there immobilized and then stuttered, "How how how does it work?"

"It has many variables and one is a GPS receiver." Gram explained.

"Ok," said Dax. "Let's go get Gunnar!"

Gram put the magic bracelet back in the box and closed the lid. The three of them all piled into Gram's BMW. As they pulled up outside of a house with the exact address, they heard many dogs barking from a building in the backyard.

Gram looked at the boys and said, "I think we should call the police and let them investigate what might be going on and we'll stay in the car with the doors locked."

"Let me call 911, Gram," Zayne said excitedly. "I know Gunnar is back there."

The two policemen arrived within 15 minutes and parked behind Gram's car. They both got out and went up to Gram's window. Gram rolled her window down and said, "My grandsons dog has been stolen and we think he is caged up in a building in this backyard." She pointed to the building where they heard the sound of barking dogs.

The policemen got out there flashlights and walked back into the shadows Gram, Dax and Zayne waited in the car patiently. After about 20 minutes the policemen appeared with two men that were handcuffed. They put the two thieves in the back seat of the squad car. One of the policeman came up to Gram's window, "Ok ma'am, those are all stolen dogs. We found the false AKC papers for each dog. All the dogs will be returned to their owners in the next few days and the two thieves will be sent to jail. I don't know how you found them, but you and your boys are so brave. Thank you." and the policeman got in his car and drove away.

Gram looked at both boys and winked, "A job well done."

Dax and Zayne both shouted out, "Thank you Magic Bracelet."

Just then out from the backyard Gunnar appeared.

"Look Gram there's Gunnar running toward us. I bet he smelled us and broke out of his cage" yelled Dax and Zayne at the same time.

They opened the car door and Gunnar jumped in the car with his tail wagging and barking for joy. Everyone was so happy they all gave hugs and eskimo kisses to Gunnar.

These are all the dogs that were stolen

Blue Nose American Bully

AKA: Nanny Dogs. Originally from England and were bred for hunting. A member of the American Pit Bull Terriers, they have a bluish colored coat and a stocky athletic body.

Weight range: 30 to 60 pounds

German Shepherd

Originated from Germany for herding and guarding sheep. One of the smartest and most popular dogs. Also trained for police rescue and service dogs for the disabled.

Weight range: 60 to 80 pounds

Yorkshire Terrier

AKA: Yorkie. Small dog breed developed in the 19th century in Yorkshire, England. Their purpose was to catch rats in the clothing mills. These little dogs make a great companion.

Hypoallergenic Weight range: 6 to 8 pounds

Dalmatian

AKA: Fire House Dog This breed originated in Croatia (Eastern Europe) and used as a carriage dog to run alongside of the carriages. Also noted for black, liver spots on their short hair coats.

Weight range: 35 to 65 pounds

West Highland White Terrier

AKA: Westie. This breed is from Scotland in the toy dog category. They have a white harsh top coat and a soft white undercoat. An excellent travel companion and easy to train.

Hypoallergenic Weight range: 13 to 22 pounds

Shih Tzu

AKA: Chinese Lion Dog. This breed originated in the Tibetan region of China. They were used for lap dogs for the Emperors of China. They need constant grooming and are very playful.

Weight range: 9 to 16 pounds

Golden Retriever

This breed originated from England and was bred for retrieving birds that were shot during hunting season. This large popular dog is easy to train and is a loyal family companion.

Weight range: 55 to 70 pounds

Chihuahua

This dog is the National symbol of Mexico from the state of Chihuahua, Mexico.

They are one of the smallest breeds and considered cuddly toy dog with a big attitude.

Weight range: 3 to 7 pounds

GLOSSARY

Acronym = An abbreviation formed from the first initial letter of each word or title.

AKA = Also Known As

AKC = American Kennel Club = A registry for pedigree dogs.

BMW = Bavarian Motor Works = A car made in Southern Germany in the Bavarian region.

GPS = Global Positioning System = A satellite navigation system used to pinpoint the ground locations of everything.

RFID = Radio Frequency Identification = This is used in the form of a wireless communication to identify an object, animal or person.

USA = United States of America

911 = A phone number called for any emergency assistance from the police, fire department or ambulance services.

DEDICATION:

Dedicated to the ones I love : My daughter, Amber Allen and my entire family.

Printed in the United States
By Bookmasters